Savann...

books are my...

Lost

Puppy

Love

Savannah,

Real heroes rea...

David...

ISBN 979-0-9846528-0-8

Printed in the U.S.A.

First Printing, September 2011

This Puppy and Potion

Demand Your Devotion

CONTENTS

Real Heroes Read!
realheroesread.com

#12: Lost Puppy Love

David Anthony
and
Charles David Clasman

Illustrations
Lys Blakeslee

Traverse City, MI

Home of the Heroes

abigail

andrew

zoë

CHAPTER 1:
MEET THE HEROES

Welcome to Traverse City, Michigan, population 18,000. The city has everything you might expect: malls, movie theaters, schools, and playgrounds. Kids swim here in the summer and build snowmen during the winter. Sometimes they pretend that they live in an ordinary place.

But Traverse City is far from ordinary. It is set on one of the Great Lakes and attracts tourists in every season. Thousands of people visit every year.

Still, few of them know the city's real secret. Even fewer talk about it. You see, Traverse City is home to three likeable superheroes. This story is about them.

Meet Abigail, the oldest of our heroes by a whole eight minutes. When it comes to sports, she can't be beat—not at lacrosse, not at the long jump, and certainly not at lumberjack events. In fact, pet owners everywhere depend on Abigail's athletic skill. Cat stuck in a pine? No need to whine. Abigail's Hairball Highjump always saves the day.

Andrew comes next. He's Abigail's twin brother, younger by a measly eight minutes. If it has wheels, Andrew can ride it. He's lightning, learned, and the law on wheels—exactly the sort of daring driver you would want in an emergency. Just ask the local animal rescue team. The last time they got a call, Andrew beat the ambulance to the racetrack.

Last but definitely not least is Baby Zoë. She's proof that big things can come in small packages. She still wears a diaper, but the Coast Guard keeps her on speed dial. Zoë puts the *leg* in *legend.*

Together these three heroes keep the streets and neighborhoods of Traverse City, Michigan, and America safe. Together they are …

CHAPTER 2:
MEET THE COPPERS

"We're on deck," Abigail informed her siblings. "Next up—us!"

Hearing the news, Andrew and Zoë shared pleased looks. It was about time! They had been waiting 15 minutes to get their fingerprints taken. Not even criminals in jail waited that long!

Zoë, however, didn't quite understand what to expect. She mistook fingerprints for a very important person. She expected to meet royalty today, a real nobleman. She expected to meet the one and only Finger Prince!

That, of course, wasn't meant to be. The heroes and the people of Traverse City had gathered to celebrate *Meet the Coppers*. Sponsored by the police, the yearly event offered games, activities, and demonstrations for the whole family. To participate, attendees had to be fingerprinted. Admission was otherwise free.

After the heroes washed the ink off their fingers, Andrew wheeled them to their first stop: a motorcycle demonstration by the Chopper Cops. The heroes' friend, Officer Duncan McDoughnut, showed off his riding skills first. He paraded past pylons, wheelied while waving, and raced 'round the crowd.

Even Andrew was grudgingly impressed by the officer's driving. "Not bad," he admitted. "For a human."

Abigail gave her brother a quizzical stare. "For a human?" she repeated. "What does that make you?"

Andrew thrust an index finger into the air, preparing to respond. *Listen up,* the gesture demanded. Zoë quickly cut him off.

"Loco," she said. Andrew was crazy. Human but crazy. Her own index finger rotated next to the side of her head.

Next in the lineup came the T.C. K9ers—Traverse City's special canine unit. These daring dogs could sniff out danger even with clothespins on their noses. Sense trouble blindfolded. Eat treats without using their paws. They even located a criminal in the crowd. Imagine the surprise!

The K9ers knew how to play too. They fetched and frolicked, barked and begged, all on command of their trainer, Officer Harry Barker.

When the officer broke out a Frisbee, Abigail couldn't resist leaping into the action. She had recently hoped to play Frisbee with a dinosaur, but that didn't work out as planned.* Trained police dogs were the next best thing. *Chomp!*

*See Heroes A²Z #4: Digging for Dinos

Abigail didn't go so far as to follow the K9ers into their kennel. After the dogs' performance, they deserved every biscuit and bone for themselves. Abigail rejoined her family instead.

She did, however, glance longingly at the dogs a last time. She also whispered one heartfelt word.

"Please?"

Andrew echoed it immediately, and Zoë clasped her tiny hands together.

"Loveable?" she begged her parents.

Mom and Dad smiled at one another before nodding. How could they refuse? Abigail, Andrew, and Baby Zoë wanted a pet. So Michigan's superhero family would adopt one.

CHAPTER 3:
PICK A PET

Most kids want a pet. It could be a typical cuddly kitten or playful puppy. Maybe a frisky ferret or a huggable hamster. Possibly a long-tailed lizard with big, buggy eyes.

It's hard to decide with all those choices. In this, the heroes were as normal as any other kids. All three of them had ideas, but they didn't agree. Mom and Dad, though, agreed on an important point.

"One family," Mom said.

"One pet," Dad finished.

The twins scowled and Zoë crossed her arms.

"Letdown," she muttered under her breath. So much for one pet per hero!

Abigail naturally made her selection first. Number one as usual. Once she and her family arrived at the pet store, she trotted straight to the turtle terrarium. She wanted an athletic sidekick with built-in armor.

"Interesting choice," Dad commented. "I assumed you would pick something speedier."

Abigail grinned slyly. "Remember the fairy tales," she said. "Turtles and I have a lot in common. We always win the race."

Andrew wound his way to the snake pit. He had his eyes and ideas on a baby boa constrictor. Another surprise choice!

Seeing the snake caused Mom to shiver. She hated snakes. She hated their slithery scales, their tricky tongues, and their eerie eyes.

"Snakes aren't round," she told her son quickly. "You ought to choose a different animal. Look for something more like a wheel."

Andrew shrugged, his own wheels turning. "I like my choice," he said. "I have a plan."

Abigail laughed from across the store. "Don't you get it, Mom? His plan is to take up the hula hoop!"

The word "hula" confused Zoë the same way fingerprints had earlier. It gave her a completely wrong mental image. One that had nothing to do with a snake or a hoop. She immediately imagined Andrew dancing. *Hula* dancing.

"Luau?" she wondered, thinking of a Hawaiian feast and the accompanying entertainment.

Andrew almost choked. "Never!" he gasped.

"You're impossible!" Andrew went on. "All of you."

Zoë shrugged, pretending to be innocent. She enjoyed annoying her brother. It was so easy! Sometimes she could barely keep from laughing at him.

"Laughing!" she repeated out loud. That was it! Zoë wanted a pet that could laugh with her.

And nothing laughed better than a hyena.

Stamp!

"That's enough," Mom said, putting down her foot. "We're going home."

"But ..." the twins protested.

Zoë's mouth fell open. "Leaving?" Her voice quivered as she asked. Going home? Without a pet?

"We can come back tomorrow morning," Mom continued. "*After* you agree on a pet."

Dad nodded. "Good idea. You three can camp out in the backyard tonight. Debate and argue all you want. But by morning, we will expect a decision."

In other words, the heroes were on the clock. They had a limited amount of time to decide and agree. What pet would they choose?

CHAPTER 4:
WESLEY THE WEREWOLF

"Listen," Zoë said, holding a finger to her lips.

She and her family were camped in the backyard. Mom and the twins were roasting marshmallows over a bonfire. Dad was preparing to tell one of his spooky stories. He called them Mystery Underground. Why? Because the spookiest mysteries were secrets and best kept hidden from all but the bravest audiences.

Dad sat on a stump on the far side of the fire. Shadows darkened his face.

"Did you know that Traverse City is haunted?" he asked. "Did you know that strange creatures inhabit Old Mission Peninsula?"

Abigail stopped roasting and snickered, unafraid. "Sure, Dad," she said. "And I'm a robo-cone robot."*

Dad ignored her. "A boy slightly older than Zoë has haunted the area for years. No one remembers his name anymore. Now they just call him the Boy with the Broken Flashlight."

Dad lowered his voice to a whisper. "Some say the boy became lost in the woods after visiting Old Mission Lighthouse. Others say that his family left him alone on purpose. They didn't want him anymore. The boy was cursed. He was a *werewolf!*"

On saying the word "werewolf," Dad jumped to his feet and revealed something from behind his back.

Zoë jumped, too, straight into the air. She shrieked, "Lycanthrope!" That was another word for werewolf.

Zoë covered her eyes and shook with fear. A werewolf? Terrifying! Nothing was worse. Monsters and villains should not look like the family dog. What a cruel trick!

Abigail placed a hand on her sister's shoulder. "Don't worry, Zoë. It's not a real werewolf. Look."

"It's just a puppet," Andrew added. "A *lame* puppet."

Sure enough, Dad wore a tattered old puppet on his right hand. It was supposed to be a werewolf, but it was so threadbare it looked like a toddler's chew toy.

"Wesley Werewolf isn't lame," Dad protested.

Abigail nodded. "Lame and maimed," she pronounced.

Slowly Zoë peeked open her eyes. "Lame?" she asked hesitantly.

Abigail nodded again. Dad wiggled his fingers, making the puppet dance. Its tiny arms and legs flopped crazily. Nothing scary there.

"See, Zoë?" Andrew said. "Lame. Besides, you know we could take care of any real werewolf. We're Heroes A²Z! We would tame the werewolf and keep it as a pet."

Zoë smiled. She liked the thought of that.

"That's enough about werewolves," Mom said. "It's time for you kids to think about other animals. You have a decision to make." She snatched the puppet from Dad to prove she meant business.

"No more Wesley Werewolf?" he asked in a fake child's voice.

Mom shook her head. "Not tonight."

"No more s'mores?" Abigail pled.

"Nope."

"Marshmallows?" Andrew tried.

"None."

The only request she couldn't deny came from Zoë. "Lullaby?" she asked.

"Of course," Mom softened. "I'll sing you a lullaby. But then Dad and I are going into the house. You three will have to choose a pet on your own."

CHAPTER 5:
SHADOW PUPPETS

Mom poked her head into the heroes' tent. "Teeth brushed?" she asked.

"Pearly white," Abigail replied, flashing a smile as proof.

"Pajamas on?" Mom continued.

Andrew pulled on his collar with a finger. "Buttoned all the way up," he said.

"Good." Mom nodded and duplicated Abigail's smile. "What's left?"

"Light," Zoë piped up. She refused to sleep without a nightlight.

A light and a lullaby it was. Afterward, Mom left the tent. The heroes lay quietly for almost a minute. None of them wanted to start arguing over pets again. Finally Abigail snickered.

"Check it out," she said. "It's a goalpost on a football field."

She held her hands and arms into the light of Zoë's battery-powered lantern. A shadow puppet appeared on the far wall of the tent.

It was a football goalpost, just like she said.

Andrew quickly removed his socks and rolled them into a ball. Rolled, ball—paying attention? The superhero of wheels was up to something round.

"The kick is up," he said, flicking his wrist. The balled socks arced over to Abigail and bonked her on the forehead.

Silly, sure, but also something else. The socks cast a shadow puppet that resembled a kicked football splitting the uprights of Abigail's goalpost.

"The kick is good!" Andrew finished. "Field goal, three points!"

Abigail caught the socks and returned them to her brother—hard and fast. He received a footwear fastball between the eyes. *Bonk!*

"Necessary roughness," she said.

"Don't you mean *unnecessary* roughness?" Andrew moped. That was the usual call in football. It meant tackling a player with too much force.

Abigail shook her head. "Not this time," she smirked. "Now let's see your shadow puppet without socks."

Andrew huffed but held up a hand to the light. On the tent wall appeared a familiar face.

"Wesley Werewolf," he said.

Bonk! Zoë tossed the socks at him again.

Andrew shot his little sister a look. "Fine, Zoë," he said. "Think you can do better?"

She nodded and climbed out of her sleeping bag. She would need all ten fingers and toes to create her masterpiece.

"Any day now," Andrew said, pulling on his socks. Better safe than sorry.

With her tongue sticking out of her mouth, Zoë managed to say, "Liberty." Her shadow puppet was ready.

Nevertheless, her siblings couldn't take their eyes off her. Zoë had tied herself into knots to form the shadow.

"Lady," Zoë mumbled, tongue still out. Her siblings had better hurry. She couldn't hold this crazy position forever.

The twins finally glanced at the tent wall. Their mouths fell open, and silence filled the tent.

Zoë had surpassed their humble shadow puppets. She was the teacher and they the students on the first day of school.

The Statue of Liberty, also called Lady Liberty, decorated their tent wall.

Andrew and Abigail almost applauded. Their sister had created a work of shadow art. They froze, however, when it seemed Zoë wasn't finished.

A new shadow took shape on the tent wall next to Lady Liberty. Small at first, it quickly grew. Limbs appeared, then a head, ears, and tail. When it opened its mouth, it displayed rows of fangs.

"How are you doing that?" Abigail whispered.

Zoë just shook her head. She wasn't. The new shadow was real. It was alive.

And it was lurking outside their tent.

CHAPTER 6:
A LOST SURPRISE

Zoë squealed and leaped into her sister's arms. Something unknown was lurking outside their tent. Something that cast a spooky shadow on the wall. What could it be?

"Calm down, Zoë," Abigail said. "It's probably just Wesley Werewolf."

She meant to comfort Zoë. Wesley was only a hand puppet. But one mention of the werewolf caused Zoë's bottom lip to quiver. Tears couldn't be far behind.

Andrew came to the rescue. "She means Dad is making the shadow. You know, he's playing a trick on us."

Zoë knotted her eyebrows together, thinking. Eventually she came up with a troubling idea.

"Liar?" she asked, meaning Dad. Wasn't tricking someone the same as lying to them?

Andrew shook his head. "No, no. Lies hurt, but tricks are fun."

"Yeah, let's play one now," Abigail grinned mischievously. "On Dad."

Zoë grinned too. She liked the sound of that.

The heroes crept from their tent on the tippiest of toes. Even Zoë's piggy toes padded across the ground. Dad would be extra surprised to see her walking instead of flying.

Abigail led her siblings around the right side of the tent. The shadow came from the left. When they reached the corner, they paused, ready to pounce on Dad. Andrew counted silently to three with his fingers. Then the heroes leaped around the corner and made their scariest faces.

Boo!

Surprise! The joke was on them. When the heroes landed, they froze in dismay. Confusion quickly replaced the spooky looks on their faces.

Zoë pointed. "Look …" she began.

"… at …" Abigail continued.

"… that!" Andrew finished, his voice a stunned whisper.

Dad wasn't behind the tent. No other human being was. Something they hadn't expected crouched in the grass.

After a silent pause, Abigail found her voice first. No surprise for the frequent winner. Delighted, she dropped to her knees.

"It's a puppy!" she squealed. "A precious little puppy!"

Zoë clapped her pudgy hands. "Labrador!"

Their actions broke Andrew's stupor. He knelt, too, and touched a finger to his lips.

"Hush," he chided his sisters. "Can't you see the puppy is scared?"

The puppy raised its head timidly. Tender brown eyes as rich and deep as dark chocolate met their gaze. They were so big and so perfectly round. They were impossible not to love.

"Help me," the puppy sniffed. "I'm lost."

CHAPTER 7:
LOVE POTION #K9

A talking dog? Incredible! The heroes stood silent, stunned, and surprised. Then—one, two, three—their mouths fell open and they started talking at the same time.

"Amazing!" Abigail admitted.

"Awesome!" added Andrew.

"Legendary!" Zoë laughed.

In the past, the three had met talking rabbits, dinosaurs, and kitties. It was about time a dog joined the list.

"I think we found our pet," Andrew said.

"Maybe he found us," Abigail countered.

Either way, the heroes finally agreed. They would not return to the pet store. They had found the newest member of their family. The lost little puppy was welcome in their home.

"Lucky!" Zoë exclaimed, feeling overjoyed. Her brother and sister took it as a suggestion. Moreover, they approved.

"Good idea," Abigail said. "We'll name him Lucky."

"Perfect," Andrew agreed. "How many dogs get adopted by superheroes?"

"Lottery," Zoë answered. Lucky barely described it. The lost puppy had won the new owner lottery.

Silently, the puppy also agreed. He was lucky, all right, but not for the reason the heroes assumed. He was lucky because his plan was working.

Now for phase two.

While the heroes congratulated each other, Lucky reached into his fur with a paw. He drew out a peculiar bottle and drank the pink liquid within. No one saw him do it.

The bottle resembled a bone-shaped dog biscuit. A cap like a Labrador's head crowned the bottle. Its label read, "Love Potion #K9" inside a red heart.

When the heroes looked at the puppy again, his eyes had changed. Gone were the gentle, deep chocolate beauties. Gone was the sweet, shy look of innocence.

Now Lucky's eyes swirled like the colorful pattern on a lollypop. Now his eyes forced the heroes to obey.

"Look into my eyes," Lucky commanded. "You love me. You do! And you will take me downtown. We have important business tonight."

The heroes nodded woodenly.

"Downtown," Andrew droned like a sleepy zombie.

"Business," Abigail babbled.

Zoë and the twins would do whatever Lucky wanted. They were under the spell of his Love Potion #K9.

CHAPTER 8:
DOUGHNUTS FOR MCDOUGHNUT

"Leash?" Zoë asked, looking at Lucky. The puppy's eyes had returned to normal, but the heroes remained under his control.

The little dog laughed, the sound part snarl and part sneer. "Never!" he declared. "Never again will dogs wear leashes or do mankind's bidding. You are the pets now, and I am the master. Sit, humans, sit. Do as I say."

The heroes dropped to their backsides and smiled at Lucky. Of course they would do as he asked. They loved him. They couldn't help themselves.

"We will travel in that," Lucky said. He pointed at an odd vehicle parked next to the curb. It was part garbage truck, part broom on wheels. It was called a street cleaner. The heroes' neighbor, Dustin Rhoades, operated the vehicle at night to keep Traverse City's streets free of debris and excess dirt.

"Taking that would be stealing," Abigail correctly pointed out. "The street cleaner doesn't belong to us."

"Look into my eyes," Lucky told her. She did, and the swirl of colors returned.

"But if it has wheels, Andrew can ride it," Abigail said. Her attitude had completely changed. "So let's climb on board!"

Abigail was right. Andrew could ride anything with wheels, even a street cleaner. That meant he could drive one too. So they piled into and onto the strange vehicle and pulled away from the curb.

"Stop!" a man's voice called out behind them. It belonged to Mr. Rhoades, the cleaner's official driver. "Come back!"

The heroes, however, didn't hear him. They continued down the road. So Mr. Rhoades pulled out his cellphone and frantically called the police.

Red and blue lights whirled when Andrew turned the corner. Officer Duncan McDoughnut had found them. His motorcycle and another officer's cruiser blocked both lanes of the street.

"I'd better pull over," Andrew said. "It's the law."

"Look into my eyes," Lucky replied from the seat next to him.

Andrew did and nodded. "Okay, I'll drive faster." Like Abigail, his attitude adjusted with one look into the puppy's eyes.

On the roof of the vehicle, Zoë squeaked and covered her eyes with her hands. "Lookout!" she wailed, thinking Andrew would ram the police.

Fortunately he didn't. Andrew cranked the steering wheel and swerved past Duncan McDoughnut and his vehicle.

Andrew's sisters barely clung to the top of the street cleaner. For once, Zoë wasn't the only hero flying. Abigail had unintentionally discovered flight too.

"Maniac!" she chastised her brother.

"Lunatic!" Zoë added.

"Turn here," Lucky ordered Andrew. "Into the college parking lot."

Northwestern Michigan College in Traverse City didn't have just one parking lot. But Andrew understood what Lucky wanted. It being summer, most college students had gone home. Every parking lot on campus would be empty and offer lots of space. Tires squealing, Andrew whipped into the nearest one.

"Now clean it!" Lucky barked. "Buff this parking lot. I want it as slippery as a waxed wood floor."

Andrew grinned. Again he knew what Lucky wanted: doughnuts to escape McDoughnut.

The street cleaner spun and whirled like Lucky's hypnotic eyes. Round and round it rotated, polishing the pavement. Soon the whole parking lot sparkled like ice and was twice as slick.

Duncan McDoughnut turned unknowingly into the lot. He hadn't given up on catching the heroes. He thought he had them cornered.

"Give him the freeze!" Lucky woofed out the window.

Zoë exhaled like a hurricane, causing the cop and his cruiser to spin helplessly. Lucky and the heroes then drove safely away.

"Later!" Zoë waved.

Where they went next, the heroes would never have guessed. Lucky directed them downtown to a tall building with a taller antenna out front.

Block neon letters proclaimed the building to be "TCTV"—Traverse City Television. It was the biggest TV station in the area, and also provided Internet, phone, and radio service. One stop, all shop.

"Time to spread the love," Lucky said, cracking his knuckles. "The lost puppy love."

CHAPTER 9:
TCTV

Andrew stared up at the building. Most of its windows were dark. The only significant light shone from the TCTV sign near the roof.

"I don't think anybody's home," he said.

Lucky smiled wickedly. "Let's make your little sister find out. Zoë! Go inside. But take this with you."

The dog reached out and pinched the back of Zoë's leg, hard.

Predictably, Zoë started to cry. She could tolerate a noogie to the noggin, but pinches *hurt*.

Still crying, Zoë floated to the front door. She didn't let the lock stop her. Lucky wouldn't allow it.

Knock-knock, she tapped on the glass. A security guard dressed in a blue uniform opened the door.

"Can I help you?" he asked. Then he noticed Zoë's tears. "What's wrong, little girl?"

Zoë looked at him and sniffed. "Lure," she explained, seeing no reason to lie. Lucky was using her as bait to catch the guard unprepared.

Tada! Abigail and Andrew leaped from behind
Zoë's back. Between them, they raised Lucky to meet
the security guard's gaze.

"Look into my eyes," the puppy commanded. His
eyes whirled like a shuffling kaleidoscope.

The security guard exhaled noisily and his body
visibly relaxed. He was clearly under the puppy's
control.

"Come in, please," he said, holding the door open
wide. "The station is yours."

Once inside, Lucky looked around suspiciously. "Who else is here?" he demanded.

The guard shrugged. "Just me," he said. "The late night shows are programmed ahead of time. Look, see? The Kung Fu Kitties* are on now." He pointed at a widescreen television mounted on the wall in the lobby.

The heroes recognized the episode immediately. "Rattlesnake Rattle Shake!" Andrew exclaimed. "I love this episode. The Rattler is pretending to be a baby."

*See Heroes A²Z #11: Kung Fu Kitties

Suddenly a siren shrieked outside, and a vehicle squealed to a stop on the street. Everyone ran to the windows.

"It's Officer Harry Barker!" Andrew reported. "And the canine unit."

Lucky rubbed his paws together. From his fur, he produced another bottle of Love Potion #K9. "Give me time to reload," he ordered. "Then I will take care of those coppers."

Abigail hesitated, confused. "Should we play Frisbee with them?"

"No, I want you to fight!" Lucky snarled. "Now get out there!"

The heroes had no choice but to obey. Lucky's hypnotic eyes controlled them. Would they ever break the puppy's spell?

CHAPTER 10:
CRIMINALS VS. COMMANDOS

Heads down, the heroes exited the TCTV building. They felt ashamed of what they had done tonight and for what they were about to do. First they had stolen the street cleaner. Then they had trapped Officer Duncan McDoughnut in the college parking lot. Now they were going to pick a fight with the police. They were acting like criminals.

Lucky's love potion had them doing the unthinkable!

"Put 'em up," Abigail said, raising her fists like a boxer. Andrew and Zoë grimly mimicked the gesture.

"Give up peacefully, kids," Officer Barker said into a megaphone. "I don't want anyone to get hurt."

Frowning, Andrew shook his head. "We can't," he replied.

"We have to do what the puppy wants," Abigail explained. "We love him."

"Lawbreakers," Zoë sniffed unhappily.

Officer Barker sighed, also unhappily. The heroes gave him no choice. He turned to his canine commandos and issued an order.

"Attack!"

The K9ers responded instantly, leaping like uncoiled springs. Snarling and barking, they charged the heroes.

Abigail acted first, reaching into her duffle bag. She snatched a Frisbee and snapped it into the air. She hoped it would distract the dogs.

No luck! The Frisbee sailed overhead and the K9ers kept coming. They were trained police dogs. A toy wouldn't prevent them from performing their duty.

"Zoë, grab my hand!" Andrew cried. He had a plan: a super spin called the Hero Hurricane. It had saved the heroes when they had been surrounded before.*

His baby sister, however, had another plan. She called it escape. She knew the K9ers couldn't bite what they couldn't catch. So she snatched her siblings by the hand and swept them toward the sky. They landed safely on the antenna outside. From there, they watched what happened next below.

*See Heroes A²Z #6: Fowl Mouthwash

66

Back on the ground, the canine unit skidded to a collective halt. The heroes had eluded them! The dogs looked to Officer Barker for new instructions. What should they do next?

Surprisingly it was Lucky who answered them.

"Look into my eyes," the puppy said, sitting on Officer Barker's shoulders.

"Do it," the policeman ordered. "Obey him. Now."

The K9ers sensed trouble immediately. They knew a bad dog when they smelled one, and Lucky stink-stank-stunk like the Grinch at Christmastime. Fur on end and ears low, they slowly backed away. Lucky was not to be trusted. Neither was Officer Barker anymore.

"Get back here," the officer shouted into his megaphone.

The dogs growled in response, turned, and fled. Lucky howled with laughter as they disappeared into the dark.

"Scaredy cats!" he cackled, the worst insult one dog could bark at another.

Lucky smiled to himself, feeling pleased. His plan was working perfectly. First he had hypnotized the heroes. Then the police. Next he would hypnotize the whole world from right here in Traverse City.

He rubbed his paws together and stared proudly at the TCTV building. It was his, all his. Soon he would use it to broadcast himself on TV, the internet, and onto cellphones. No one would be able to resist him. Everyone would look into his eyes. Everyone would love him.

CHAPTER 11:
A.R.F. ANTENNA

"Get to work," Lucky snapped. He clutched Officer Barker's megaphone now. "You have jobs to perform."

He was talking to the heroes, of course. Lucky had assigned tasks to each of them. Taking over TCTV had been just the first item on his terrible to-do list.

"Hurry!" he barked.

Zoë blasted off, one fist thrust above her head. The ground receded and the full moon grew larger. She was speeding into space.

Gulp!

Zoë swallowed a big breath then accelerated out of the atmosphere. Stars replaced the clouds in the sky. Darkness filled everything in between.

She was in outer space for the second time in her life!* Had Zoë not already been holding her breath, she would have stopped breathing.

She had no time to marvel, though, and went quickly to work. Not even a superhero in a diaper could hold her breath forever.

Her job was to reposition the satellites orbiting the Earth. Doing so would help Lucky take control of the airwaves.

*See Heroes A²Z #1: Alien Ice Cream

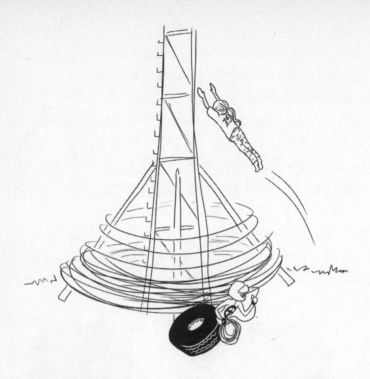

Meanwhile back on Earth, Lucky ordered the twins to modify the TCTV antenna. To do so, Andrew and Abigail combined their superpowers. Together they created the A.R.F. Antenna—the All Receiver Friendly Antenna. Not surprisingly, Lucky invented the new name.

Flipping like a gymnast on the parallel bars, Abigail ascended the antenna. Along the way, she pushed and pulled, making changes to the structure as she climbed. Andrew supported her as Kid Roll, his superhero alter ego. His secret identity! He circled the base of the antenna, winding wires from top to bottom.

When complete, the A.R.F. Antenna stood twice as tall as the original. In fact, it stood literally head-and-shoulders taller than the TCTV building. How, you ask? By having an actual head and actual shoulders.

You see, the heroes loved Lucky so much that they wanted him to know. So they designed the antenna to look like him.

Zoë finished moving the satellites at dawn and returned wearily to Traverse City. She glanced at the A.R.F. Antenna and said, "Likeness." The resemblance between the antenna and Lucky was unmistakable.

Next, Lucky sent her flying off with an advertising banner tied around her ankles. She was a commercial comet! She glided over Gladwin, flew through Fremont, soared around Southfield, and coasted around Caseville. The people in the cities and streets below read the words on her banner:

Lucky's Law @ Noon. Watch or Be Watched.

In case anyone missed seeing Zoë, Andrew acquired the TCTV news van. He hit the highway and used his powers to take an advertising adventure. He started by driving down I-75, deep into the midst of Michigan. Then he motored into Maumee, Ohio. Cruised through Crown Point, Indiana. And glided all over the Great Lakes region.

All the while, Abigail accurately tossed fliers out the windows. They bore the same words as Zoë's banner: *Lucky's Law @ Noon. Watch or Be Watched.*

For their hard work, Lucky rewarded the heroes with silver. He hung it around their necks.

"What's this?" Abigail inquired.

"Hey, stop it!" Andrew objected.

Zoë wailed one word in bewildered disbelief. *"Locks!"*

That's right. Lucky's silver reward for the heroes came in the form of chains and collars. The heroes were tied up like bad dogs and left outside a doghouse in the middle of a secluded woods.

CHAPTER 12:
LOOK INTO MY EYES

At 11:59 am, everything went black. Every TV, computer, cellphone, and device with a screen. All black, totally dark.

A minute passed in digital darkness. Then Lucky's face appeared on the screens and monitors. He wore a buttoned navy suit and a red power tie. His eyes whirled with the power of Love Potion #K9.

"Look into my eyes, America," he spoke directly into the camera filming him. "You love me and you are mine. You will do whatever I command."

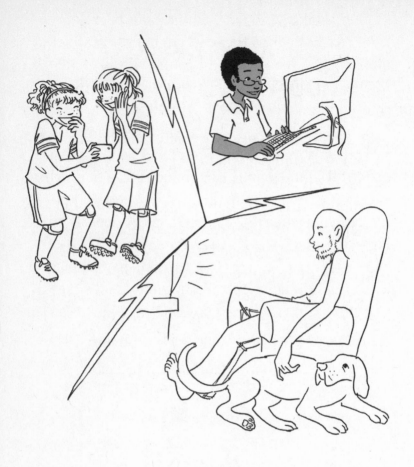

People all across America nodded in agreement. Yes, they loved the puppy. Yes, they would obey.

"He's so cute!" squealed sisters from South Carolina.

"Handsome," Californians confirmed.

"Nothing wrong with loving a dog," mused a man from Montana.

Lucky paused briefly in his speech. He smiled like a wolf before continuing. "Humans are now a dog's best friend," he said slowly. "Do for dogs as they once did for you."

He smiled again, knowing what would happen next. Humans everywhere scrambled to obey. Even the heroes' own parents were under the spell. Mom snatched her slippers. Dad grabbed the *Record Eagle*, Traverse City's hometown newspaper.

What made either of those events strange or unusual? The *way* Mom and Dad did them. The pair fetched the items in their mouths!

In fact, all of America went to the dogs. Humans and canines traded places from sea to swapping sea. Once pets, dogs now walked *their* humans.

Dogs also cared for humans the way humans had cared for them.

Many humans now worked for dogs. Some pulled
sleds.

Others served as leader humans for the blind.

The heroes, however, weren't given new jobs. They were given a new house instead. A shabby, dilapidated doghouse in the middle of the woods.

Zoë took one look at it and groaned. "Luxurious," she said sarcastically.

Lucky ignored the comment. "Sit, humans, sit," he commanded. "You're going to be here for a long, long time." Then he crawled into the doghouse and disappeared.

CHAPTER 13:
IN THE DOGHOUSE

Abigail tugged on the collar around her neck. Her human collar, as Lucky called it, itched. Yesterday the same collar would have been worn by a dog.

"I could probably slip out of it," she noted.

"Yeah, and Zoë should be able to break hers," Andrew replied.

Coulds and *shoulds,* however, didn't free them. The heroes remained captive because they refused to act.

"But Lucky wouldn't want us to escape," Andrew said.

Abigail nodded. "I love him too much to try."

Suddenly a new voice drifted out from the doghouse. It sounded sad, lonely, and utterly hopeless.

"I have the same problem," it confessed.

The heroes' eyes widened in surprise. Lucky wasn't the only one in the doghouse. From the sound of it, he had captured another prisoner. Who could it be?

"Lad?" Zoë wondered, squinting into the darkness.

Sure enough, a boy crawled slowly out of the doghouse. He wore a dirty T-shirt and shorts but no shoes. He looked a couple of years older than Andrew and Abigail. His scruffy hair needed to be brushed. He raised a hand halfheartedly and waved.

"Hi, I'm Wesley," he greeted them.

Andrew blinked. That named sounded familiar, especially coming from a lost boy in the woods.

"You're Wesley the Werewolf!" Andrew guessed.

The boy smiled glumly. "Not exactly," he said. "I prefer to be called Wes."

"But you don't mind being called a werewolf?" Abigail interjected.

Wes shrugged. "Not much I can do about it. My dog is the one causing all the trouble."

"Your dog?" Abigail asked.

"A Labrador?" Andrew pressed.

"Little?" Zoë specified.

"Yep, that's him," Wes confirmed. "Worst pet ever. I'm sorry I brought him home."

Wes sighed heavily, lost in thought. Lucky had always been a bad dog. Wes didn't know where to start. Finally he let it all out.

"Most dogs chew on toys," he began. "Lucky experimented on mine."

"He rooted for the bad guys in movies."

"He read only books written by criminals."

"And on Halloween, he dressed up like that supervillain spaceman Benjamin Axe."

"So Lucky has been bad since birth," Abigail concluded.

"Then why did you keep him?" asked Andrew.

Wes's grimy face reddened. "For the same reason you refuse to escape. I love that dog. I can't disobey him."

Silence followed Wes's confession. The heroes knew exactly how he felt. They couldn't disobey Lucky either. At least not until his Love Potion #K9 wore off.

And none of them knew how long that would be.

CHAPTER 14:
THE LABRADOR'S LAB

Helpless, hopeless, and hapless. That was how the heroes felt. In the past, they had been tied up, locked down, put out, and taken in by villains. But never before had they been unable to at least *try* to escape. The love they felt for Lucky was stronger than a prison. It kept them from doing anything to help themselves.

For one of the few times ever, the heroes needed a hero.

So where were the men of steel? The caped crusaders? The captains dressed in underpants?

Apparently those kinds of heroes hid in the woods, because Zoë heard someone approaching from the trees. Her head came up and she touched a finger to her lips.

"Listen," she hissed.

Abigail, Andrew, and Wes held their breath. All eyes focused on the trees in front of the doghouse. All ears strained to hear …

Dogs barking.

"Bummer," Andrew muttered. "Lucky's friends are coming."

Good guess, but wrong. Because from the trees pounced a pack of dogs, and not one of them liked Lucky, much less loved him.

It was the Traverse City Canine Unit. The K9ers! On their backs rode another surprise—Mom and Dad!

1.
2. Lucky
3. family
4. USA
5. fighting crime before bedtime
6. books
7. video games
8. summer vacation
9. dessert
10. Princess and Rabbit

Baby Zoë and the twins cheered. Talk about heroes for heroes! Mom and Dad rightfully topped that list.

"Remove those collars," Mom told them.

"You aren't prisoners anymore," Dad said.

And to the heroes' astonishment, it worked. They removed their collars. They were not prisoners.

"How?" Andrew and Abigail gasped, eyes agape.

Zoë placed her hands over her heart. She knew the answer. "Loyalty," she explained. The heroes loved Lucky, but they loved Mom and Dad more. Their parents were number one on every list.

"You guys rock!" Abigail exclaimed, hugging her parents.

"But we've got to roll," Andrew said. "It's puppy-payback time."

Free from Lucky's love potion, the heroes hurriedly ducked into the doghouse. It was much bigger inside than it looked outside. A narrow stone staircase descended steeply to a dungeon-like door.

"Labyrinth?" Zoë speculated, wondering just how big the doghouse was. Could it be a sprawling underground maze?

Abigail opened the door. It creaked slowly inward, revealing a brightly lit room. Test tubes and glass beakers lined polished silver shelves along the walls. Metal worktables formed a horseshoe shape around a black iron vat as big as a witch's cauldron. In the vat bubbled a familiar pink liquid—Love Potion #K9.

Zoë recognized this type of room immediately. "Laboratory," she whispered. A scientist's lab! This was where Lucky concocted his powerful potions.

A collection of full bottles proved the hypothesis. Their labels told the heroes more than any of them wanted to know. There were numerous potions that caused a variety of effects, as if they'd fallen into Alice's Wonderland.

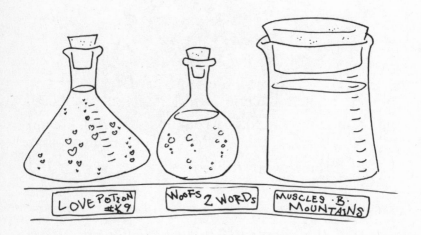

Suddenly a door on the other side of the lab opened. Lucky strode in, a grin on his furry face.

"Welcome to my science lab," he greeted the heroes.

"Don't you mean *mad* science?" Andrew challenged him.

Still grinning, Lucky shrugged. "One dog's madness is another dog's genius. Here, let me show you."

He snatched a potion bottle from the nearest worktable and twisted it open. A sharp crack of thunder boomed through the lab. That tiny bottle packed a punch!

"Prepare to be amazed," Lucky said, raising the potion in a mock toast. "I brewed this potion just for you."

CHAPTER 15:
MAD SCIENCE

Lucky raised the potion above his head. "Stand back!" he cried. "Here comes danger!"

"Stop!"

"No!"

"Letup!"

The heroes protested without success. Lucky raised the potion higher, but made no effort to drink it. He didn't even aim for his mouth. He poured the potion onto his head instead.

Had the mad scientist given up on science? Was mad all that he had?

Next the puppy started to shake. Not a simple shiver or a flinch of fear. He shook like a wet dog emerging from Lake Michigan. Can you say, *shake it, don't quake it?*

Drops and drips of potion splattered on nearby tables and equipment. So did something else.

Something that moved.

Something alive.

Abigail grabbed her sister's arm. "Fleas!" she yelped. "Don't let them near you."

Andrew laughed. "Fleas, little? Try teeny tiny. We'll roll right over them."

But as he spoke, something strange happened. The fleas started to grow. First the size of freckles, the fleas rapidly expanded. They made popping sounds like popcorn in a microwave and became as big as tiger beetles.

From tiger beetles to another kind of beetle: *Volkswagen beetles!* The fleas grew to the size of cars.

Behind them, Lucky howled and barked one word: "Attack!"

CHAPTER 16: FLEA FORCE

The average flea can leap 150 times its height. Imagine a person doing that. That human flea could leap over a skyscraper.

So when Lucky ordered his flea force to attack, the fleas did what they do best. They jumped. Onto the heroes. And then they jumped again.

SMASH!

Up through the ceiling with the heroes in their clutches.

The heroes and fleas sped up and up. They passed the brown of the ground, the green of trees, and into the blue beyond. To the heroes, the flight felt like falling into the sky. All three hoped to land in a cloud, of course.

The fleas, on the other hand, had different hopes. Namely, they hoped to be rid of the heroes. So when they reached the heights of their hops, some of them let go.

Andrew and Abigail fell, screaming. Zoë watched them drop. A swarm of fleas still clutched her. She could do nothing to help her siblings.

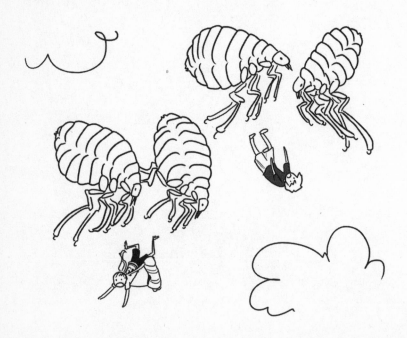

Abigail's stomach leaped into her throat. Her hands dipped into her bag. Her duffel bag, that is. The one she kept handy at all times, and the one that contained every piece of sports equipment imaginable. Even the kind that require a lot of imagination to imagine.

Out she plucked a basketball, a kickball, and a soccer ball. No luck or help there. Next she scored a diving board, a saddle, and a scuba mask. Useful, maybe, if she were going to tame a seahorse.

"Do you have a helicopter in that bag?" Andrew howled. "Anything that can fly?" He knew that every moment falling was a moment closer to landing.

To *crash* landing.

"Silly me!" Abigail snapped in response. "I was looking for gravity boots or rocks to put in my pockets."

Andrew brightened instantly. "Boots! That's it! Well, shoes actually. I'm wearing my inflatable skatables."*

He confidently clicked his heels together. Big, balloon-like tires inflated from the soles of his tennis shoes.

"One soft, safe landing coming up," he announced like the pilot of a plane.

*See Heroes A²Z #8: Holiday Holdup

If only it were that easy.

Chomp!

The fleas didn't like Andrew's plan. They liked his inflatable shoes less. In mid-fall, they flew in close and bit his tennis shoe tires.

Pop!

So much for that soft, safe landing.

In frustration, Abigail flipped over her duffel bag and shook it. Various pieces of sports equipment tumbled out—a golf bag, ski boots, boxing gloves, and a swimmer's cap. Nothing that would help.

"Brace yourself!" she cried. A crash landing seemed unavoidable. Seemed all but certain.

With a clank, the duffel bag crashed to the ground. Abigail and Andrew landed on top of it. The pair expected a thump and to be flattened like pancakes. Instead they bounced gently off the bag.

Boing!

Why? Because the duffel bag wasn't empty. Among other things, a personal mini-trampoline remained within it. The twins high-fived in mid-air, astounded by their luck.

Zoë, however, wasn't so fortunate. The fleas clutching her didn't let go. They knew she could fly and that dropping her would be pointless. So they plunged to the ground without trying to slow.

BOOM!

Zoë and the fleas crashed to Earth like a meteorite. Dirt and rocks exploded. Dust filled the air. The noise of a thunderclap ripped through the woods. The impact knocked everyone in the area to the ground.

Could Zoë survive a landing like that?

CHAPTER 17:
K9 COLLARS

"My baby!" Mom wailed.

"Zoë?" the twins called.

None of them could see through the dust in the air.

"Say something, Zoë," Dad pleaded. "Can you hear us? Are you okay?"

The dust slowly settled, revealing a hole in the ground that hadn't been there before. The hole was deep, dark, and shaped exactly like Zoë.

The twins, their parents, the K9ers, and Wes gathered around the Zoë-shaped hole. They peered inside, hoping, waiting, and holding their breath.

Covered in dirt, Zoë finally emerged. She pulled her upper torso over the rim of the hole and leaned heavily on her elbows.

"Locomotive," she mumbled. Zoë felt as if she'd been hit by a train.

The humans cheered and the K9ers yipped happily. Zoë was banged and bruised but alive.

All of them were so relieved, in fact, that they did not sense the coming danger. No one noticed the fleas surrounding them. Not until it was too late.

"Legion," Zoë warned.

The battle was about to begin … again.

The K9ers responded first and fastest. They had a natural dislike for fleas. They also had an unnatural defense against them—a secret weapon worn around their necks.

Flea collars.

Now it was the K9ers' turn to jump. Directly onto the fleas. They jumped, the fleas fell, and the dogs pinned them with their collars.

After that the heroes hogtied the fleas. One collar per customer, one flea after another.

Zoë finally floated out of the hole. She wore a big grin on her little face.

"Laughingstock," she teased the fleas. Once again good had triumphed. Bad guys were such a joke!

"Don't plan a party yet," a voice growled behind Zoë. Startled, she and the others turned.

Lucky met their gaze. He stood defiantly on the rubble surrounding the Zoë-shaped hole. In one paw he clutched a full potion bottle. In the other, a spiked leather collar.

"Give it up," Abigail told him.

"It's over, dog," Andrew said.

Lucky shrugged them off. "If you want something done right, do it yourself," he said. Then, with a sneer, he slapped the spiked collar around his neck and drank the potion dry.

As everyone watched, the puppy started to change.

CHAPTER 18:
BEEFCAKE BRUTE

As soon as he swallowed the last drop of potion, Lucky began to grow. His chest expanded. His arms thickened. Muscles even rippled along his tail.

"Lumberjack!" Zoë gasped. The cuddly, loveable puppy was now a beefcake brute.

Lucky howled and flexed his new massive upper body muscles.

"That's exactly what I was thinking," he told Zoë. "Watch this!"

The burly dog wrapped his bulky arms around a nearby oak tree and pulled. *Crack!* The tree snapped, breaking clean, and Lucky raised it over his head. Only a stump remained on the ground.

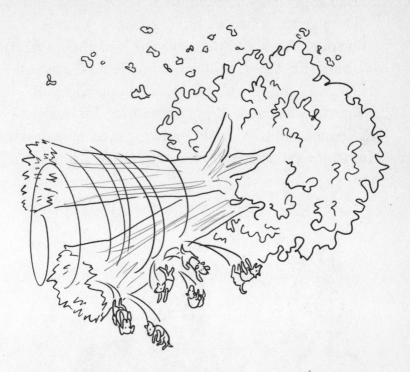

Lucky was as strong as Zoë now. His muscles had muscles. His arms had attitude.

"Let's see which is worse," he snarled. "My bark or my bite."

But before he could say more, the K9ers charged. They wielded barks and bites, too, which usually beat their opponents.

Strike!

Not this time. Lucky lurched forward and heaved the oak tree into the oncoming dogs. It struck head-on, scattering the K9ers like bowling pins.

Bark 1, Bite 0. *Tree* bark, that is.

"Bad dog!" Abigail exclaimed.

"Do you see what you did?" accused Andrew.

Furious, the twins transformed into their secret superhero identities. Abigail became Triple-A, the All-American Athlete. Andrew rounded into Kid Roll.

Then they charged, daring Lucky to try his tree trunk trick again. Triple-A would leap a log in a single stride. Kid Roll would shred it like a buzz saw. Bring it on, puppy!

Seeing them coming, Lucky snarled and pawed the ground like an angry bull. He dropped to all fours. He lowered his head. He charged.

Three could play that game!

Crash!

Heroes and hound collided. Their bodies smacked, the impact cracked, and for a moment the three saw only black.

Andrew bounced high away, landing in a tangle of branches above. A family of bald eagles, America's national bird and symbol, looked as surprised as he did.

Abigail plowed into a pine headfirst. Like Winnie-the-Pooh after eating too much honey, she poked half-in and half-out, wholly stuck. But instead of a rabbit, two shocked squirrels shook their furry fists at her.

As for Lucky, he just laughed. The expression "muscle head" existed for a reason. Not because of brains but because of brawn. And the expression described Lucky since he'd lapped his latest potion. His hard head was stuffed with muscles. Running into the heroes hadn't hurt him at all.

The powerful puppy stood, dusted himself off, and flexed his upper body again. "Who's next?" he challenged. "Who dares to face Lumberjack Lucky?"

CHAPTER 19:
PUPPY LOVE LOST

Lucky raised his thick arms in triumph. He had clobbered the K9ers and toppled the twins. That left only Baby Zoë to oppose him.

"Give it your best shot," he taunted her.

Zoë nodded grimly and started to advance. Still dizzy from her crash landing, she knew her current best wouldn't be full strength.

"Lassitude," she complained to herself. She was already exhausted while Lucky was unnaturally strong.

The two combatants clashed like wrestlers in the ring. Their bodies crashed together. Their arms and legs grasped and grappled for advantage.

When their eyes met, Lucky growled. "I'm going to bury you in a backyard," he declared.

"Lesson," Zoë shot back, as in what she was going to teach him.

Their battle continued. Lucky earned the first takedown, driving Zoë to her knees.

"Our baby!" Mom and Dad cried from the sidelines.

Zoë fought back by flipping Lucky over her head. He landed with a mighty thud.

"My puppy!" Wes wailed.

Almost forgotten by everyone, Lucky's owner Wes flew into the fray. He knelt next to Lucky and held up one hand, ordering Zoë to stop.

"You're going to hurt him!" Wes whined. "Leave Lucky alone. I love him!"

Zoë paused, confused. Wes remained under the spell of Love Potion #K9. Could he be trusted? Should she listen to him?

Those questions were never answered.

Lucky glanced at Wes and curled his lips in disgust. "Get your hands off me, human," he snarled. Then he swatted Wes with one powerful paw and sent the boy flying.

Splash!

Into the vat of Love Potion #K9 in Lucky secret lab. The fleas, remember, had burst through the ceiling. The lab—and the vat—were open to the world above ground.

As they had done earlier, the humans and canines gathered around a hole. Not Zoë's this time. The hole in the lab's ceiling. They watched as Wes dragged himself out of the vat below. He was soaking wet, completely drenched. He coughed one, sneezed twice, and then opened his eyes.

His swirling, hypnotic eyes.

He spotted Lucky in the crowd. "You love me, Lucky," he said. "You love me and you will do what I say."

Lucky sighed, unable to resist. He was under Wes's control now. He had been hypnotized by his own potion!

"Surrender," Wes told him, and Lucky did so without argument. He calmly held up his paws for the Traverse City Canine Unit and waited to be handcuffed.

"Victory!" Abigail cheered from the pine. "Now how about pulling me out?"

Farther overhead, Andrew called down. "I could use that mini-trampoline again."

Both remained stuck in trees.

After the twins had been rescued and Lucky arrested, the heroes returned to TCTV. They had unfinished business at the television station.

"Lighting?" Zoë worried, touching a hand to her hair.

"You look great, Zoë," Abigail promised. "You're on in one … two … three!"

"Rolling!" Andrew announced, operating the TV camera.

Zoë looked straight into the lens and cleared her throat. She raised Lucky's prison mug shot for the audience to see.

"Lout," Zoë said, nodding at the picture of Lucky. Telling and showing America what Lucky really was would un-hypnotize everyone who had fallen under his spell.

The heroes, in fact, were so un-hypnotized that they even forgot about wanting a pet of their own. Instead they started work on a special project: a monster truck for Andrew. Nothing could go wrong there, right? Nothing, that is, until a dangerous opponent revealed himself in …

Book #13:
Monkey Monster Truck

Fighting Crime Before Bedtime

Connect with the Authors

Charlie:
charlie@realheroesread.com
facebook.com/charlesdavidclasman

David:
david@realheroesread.com
facebook.com/authordavidanthony

realheroesread.com

facebook.com/realheroesread
youtube.com/user/realheroesread
twitter.com/realheroesread

About the Illustrator
Lys Blakeslee

Lys graduated from Grand Valley State University in Michigan where she earned a degree in Illustration.

She has always loved to read, and devoted much of her childhood to devouring piles of books from the library.

She lives in Wyoming, MI with her wonderful parents, two goofy cats, and one extra-loud parakeet.

Thank you, Lys!